AF425905

Approved by the Environmental Protection Agency

Bence Bognár

Approved by the Environmental Protection Agency

First edition. October 24, 2022.

Written by Bence Bognár

CONTENTS

Infraction

After a detour, it is always harder to return. The movie is beginning soon, and this cinema's not in a mall. The snacks that we inelegantly brought with ourselves could only be acquired by leaving the building, and this is why we are now somewhere out back in Buda's Pest-like side, the Danube-bank of District Eleven, not moneyed hills, but rather the exceedingly metropolitan energy, currently taking a left turn from the avenue into the slightly less than averagely commercial off-street. But it is sort of our fault for going to this art cinema to see a movie that's probably also played in a CinemaCity or somewhere similar, given that one finds the right one and the right time. There's bottled water and paper-wrapped biscuits in the plastic bag with the supermarket's logo on it – we had specifically bought the cheap saltines with the cardboard packing, so that the rustle of plastic wouldn't bother fellow film enthusiasts (still, we do feel a bit of shame for bypassing the crucial step of the concession stand, even though it truly is overpriced, and not even that good, and consumer culture, etcetera).

According to Google Maps, we can go through here, I say out loud, despite that visibly and obviously not being the case. A large residential building in neo-classicist style stands in our way, with a small (and already closed) photo gallery in the bottom. We've gone too much this way to turn back, and the next detour, returning to the avenue and continuing on forward, would take far too long, so after a moment of static nothingness, we look at each other and continue towards the closed private park on the left side of the building in total agreement. We have to pretend like we belong here, I say, I saw it in a video that for example with a ladder, you can get inside any establishment, even banks, but even without one, we manage to casually stroll inside before the receptionist's very eyes. He doesn't react to us at all, only focusing on his newspaper. He's an old man, looks like some sort of retired military person, he probably has more on his mind than us.

I don't know if we can get out on the other side, I hear from behind me, you are entitled to your opinion, I say, I'm already sweating, why is it so hot on an autumn night anyway, this reminds me of Sándor Weöres' poem, The Brambleberry. "Eves of autumn, Gleam with the brambleberry's, Gleam with the brambleberry's, Shimm'ring dress." That's how it goes. If I've been informed correctly, he actually had some variation of bipolar disorder, but I heard that from some literary hobby-critic in person and not a reputable source, anyway, that's one way my generation can relate to him (maybe the only one, though I'd doubt that). I gleam too, like the plant in the poem, even though it would be a bit of an overstatement to call this "eve." At least it is, in fact, of autumn. I don't look back.

It was actually my idea to take a shortcut in the first place, and people usually don't argue with me when it's about directions, but I have to admit that I screwed up. I don't make eye contact with the employees of the local restaurant, who are standing out here in the park, near a building's back door. Two of them are smoking, three of them aren't, they all stare in our direction, but we don't look at them. We turn right in a 45-degree angle, we see the place of the exit, or rather, the fence where an exit is supposed to be located, but which is devoid of it, we also see the Danube, this is what they usually call "so close yet so far away," if I'm correct. We can still turn right, go behind the building. Or more like in front of it, since now the fence is the only thing separating us from the quay, but nobody pays any attention to us, as we furtively step over the overturned cones, placed there likely over a month ago. The cordon once connecting them is long gone.

Change rattles in my pocket, I just sank it in there hastily, we were in too much of a hurry for me to put it inside my wallet, I simply grabbed the 150 forints while I was leaving the self-checkout machine at the store, and stuffed the coins into my left front pocket, where they currently are, dirtying my earphones – when to get a bacterial infection, if not now? I've already decided that I wouldn't be asking for the price of the biscuits back, by the way. My treat.

I accelerate, the movie officially begins this minute, but for now, there are probably only trailers and commercials running. Though there are always fewer of them in places like these, and they therefore obviously struggle to exist, what a stupid venue choice this was anyway, and that's my fault as well, whose would it be, I'm the one constantly dictating the programme. Actually, what I want to achieve with my current acceleration is for him to fall behind so that I could politely wait up, but he keeps up the pace, we have to turn right soon, but he probably knows that already, I tell him anyway, and he does, in fact, know, what a shocker, and he mentions how cool the RGB lights are on the building opposite to us, on the Pest side, but I don't particularly care (and what a piece of shit I am, Jesus Christ, I think, as I nod, as if noting what he had just said), my entire face is red due to the heat and the humiliation and I think that the movie had already begun.

Maybe we should run, he says, and relievedly getting pulled out of my headspace, now I genuinely do want to do that, but I know that afterward, I would be disgusting and sweaty, and instead I tell him that the commercials are probably still going on, and he doesn't answer, like he knows that not even I believe that. Then I begin to run after all, and he follows behind, he even passes me once, then mostly stays next to me, and I don't look his way, but I still imagine that he is a bit more satisfied than before, and for now, that concept is enough for me. We reach the gate and the paved pedestrian street leading through the park, and I disappointedly state that we could have gone through this area in a completely legal way, if we had just gone to the right on the street parallel to the avenue, instead of to the left and towards the reception.

We both stop running, and I begin laughing, but not in a proper and pleasing way, but almost asthmatically, and it immediately turns into coughing, and for some reason I want a scarf around my neck, even though it's still too warm here. I want it mostly for comfort. I could hide my moist face, for instance. We are irresponsibly slow, walking on the riverside, neither of us are talking, instead, we just breathe heavily. I feel something weird in my chest, and for a moment I fear that I will get the most pathetic cardiac arrest of all time right here and now, from about 100 metres of jogging, but I instantly realise that this is not anything of the sort, but something cerebral, a piercing spear of irrationality inside one's torso.

He doesn't know anything about that. Well, I mean, him not knowing anything about it at all is sort of a worst-case scenario, but it's always important to stay prepared for those. My mother always used to tell me that.

We barge into the cinema, with a sudden increase in intensity, as we both sense the finish nearing. We show our tickets, stammering, and the person checking them is so surprised that they don't even dare ask what's in our bags, although it's probably not really about daring or not, they simply don't have enough time, because we quickly march inside the auditorium. The bag is actually made of hardened plastic, I realize, so we are going to rustle either way. A shame, since we had planned this whole "model citizen" thing so well. Oh well.

We were maybe five minutes late, and there is already some dialogue going on. We sit down after finding our seats (I sit on his right), dodging the moderately damning glances. Two minutes later, not a single person inside this room will remember us at all, I try to calm myself, the movie is hopefully more interesting, and they don't care about us, as people, either way.

I decide to quickly rip off the metaphorical band-aid, and get the snacks out of the plastic bag, if not every single person here hates me in this moment, I think, then I can practically do anything for the remainder of my entire life. I stick out his rations in his face's direction, he takes them while also staring at the screen, already attempting to make sense of what is going on. He's trying to find any plot element he could connect to, or anything that piques his interest, really. My breathing is only beginning to stabilise now, but the pace of my heartbeat does not return to normal. I'm sweating like a pig. Some sort of avant-garde Latin American movie, two characters are having a tense talk on a beach. We have successfully managed to miss the beginning of the exposition. I'll get it through context anyway.

Table Tennis

As I breathe in the particles of sweat evaporating from the sticky vinyl ground, not cleaned for a month at least, the lights turn off in the corridors outside. All other rooms and kiosks on the fourth floor serve as storage space or old, dusty offices for money-laundering proxy companies. This inexplicable sport club's owner is the only renter who still keeps people inside after 6 PM, and a mall like this has to cut corners. Every surface within the training hall is different sickly shades of green: the walls are decaying mint, the vinyl on the floor is almost gray from the cheap sneakers' years of smoothening, the curtains are hospital-coloured. The tables' tint cannot really be explained, they are more integral to this whole thing than anyone not present could ever imagine.

Those who are, though, have gotten used to it already; there are only a few of them and they've had enough time. The coach is training a third-grader at the table next to ours, and I'm playing the actual game. The real deal. I've completely blocked out the other person's face, after the first lost game that becomes a necessity. Afterwards, I will re-learn the things which need forgetting for now. The match is even, two to two, and I am in the process of losing the last game, significantly so. My mind has already began wandering, possibly due to earlier complacency, or maybe I just haven't slept this time either, but the flickering of the single worn-out old LED right in front of me is incredibly distracting.

The ball bounces back and forth, creating a repetitive, monotone sound, pushing me into some sort of trance, or similar state, the dual thud of plastic first on rubber and then metal, alternating until someone finally blunders. The two sounds are supposed to be quite different in theory, but are, in fact, surprisingly similar, even if only in a sensory sense. Currently, I depend on this sport, which makes me, once again, wonder about how the mall's managers even allowed this place to be here in the first place. I lose the rally due to excessive thinking. Maybe if I had an attention span, now wouldn't that just be silly? Seems and sounds plain absurd.

I catch a glimpse of the other guy's face, still not recognizing him (my brain blurs out all past memories, thank God for that ability), yet I still can't help but realize that he is a boy my age. I probably know him, or at least his name, logically speaking. Needless to say, I absolutely do not need this thought right now. His expression determined and dumb, he focuses on one thing only, and I probably look similar right now. See, that's where I lose: when I start thinking about myself. For some reason, I have not said the score out loud after every point since about five minutes past the start of this game, like I have done in the beginning. I'm not even counting points anymore, and I really hope that he is. But, ah shit, I'm humanizing him again, aren't I? That precisely is the one thing I should not be doing. My hand trembles, and I let out a sigh. Maybe it'll distract him, but it certainly does me in for the next rally as well.

Back and forth it goes again. My brain is working against my right arm. Bicep, elbow, wrist, tricep, repeating over and over, that is the only way everything can still be fixed, but my brain really wants me to figure out why I am so tired, so I begin to involuntarily recollect last night (a miserable one). Well, my brain might be punishing me for my habits, but it's technically doing it to itself, after all. I think briefly about how this might be a form of self-harm, but the thought scares me enough that I banish it into some dark, dusty, cobweb-covered corner. No, it's definitely not an issue that I have, just a negative personality trait. And even so, I'm playing the game right now. That's what matters, I try to tell myself, but at this point I'm just lying. I haven't been in this game mentally for a while now.

But I really want to be. I want to focus on what's going on. For one rally, I try to do it the textbook way, and fail miserably – the ball is caught in the net, shot down softly, like hunting ducks with a pillowcase. I want to kick the table's leg until either it breaks, or my foot does. The table's frame is made out of solid steel: take a wild guess which'll happen first. I want to throw the racket at someone's head, so that I can research the difference in the sounds a plastic ball makes when making contact with the racket's rubber coating, as opposed to a skull's with skin used as veneer of its own. And here I am, thinking about myself. What did I just think about that? Either way, it's overshadowed by the fact that I want to chew gum, and also drink alcohol and sleep but not really and I want to not feel so God-damn alone in this green waiting room of the devil and I want to forego all my anxieties while also continue working to solve them and I want the world to end but not in the lame asteroid kind of way like the dinosaurs but the cool old testament way those ancient Jews and early Christians had a certain style I have to give them that and I want to go home and read and acquire a Lovecraftian paper tube that is usable as a spy-glass into a world of unimaginable terror and I want to fuck and I want to eat paper tissues and I want to win this mediocre match of this mediocre sport which I love. Just let me have this, whoever it is that decides.

I'm not breathing, that's apparent. This is not asthma. I fall down on my knees, heaving, other people's sweat now coating my lower legs and the inside of my lungs alike, so this is what a real panic attack feels like, this isn't one of those phony bullshit ones from before, this is the real deal, baby.

The coach hands me a bottle of water, freshly opened, he's a nice guy, but I can't drink yet, and I still do nonetheless. It is better. I wipe my eyebrows and pick up the ball. My opponent looks at me, perplexed, and proclaims that I've already won the game. He has been holding his hand out for me to shake it.

I still serve.

Serenity at Two O'clock

I put the map away. Maybe it would be helpful if I had learned how to use one of those military compasses when I had the chance, but the knowledge wouldn't be useful anyway, since I hadn't brought one to the hike. Surely, had I known how to use it, I probably would have also remembered to bring one, but that's crying over spilt milk at this point. I take the map out again, then I put it away once more.

I'm currently not following any marked path, but the main issue is that it's not even a thick forest that stands in my way, only grassy hills, covered in little spots of forestry. Because of that, I understand even less how the fuck I had managed to get this lost.

I get going as the fog covers the valley completely. I can't really value its otherworldly beauty, since, in terms of self-orientation, it really isn't helping my case. I take my phone out. I could call someone. But how could any morsel of pride remain within me if I did that? It's only ten in the morning. If I start walking in any given direction, eventually I will find some sort of settlement. Of course, I haven't left the car in all of them at once, and I'm not particularly aware of how local public transport works, but at least I can make sure that I don't freeze to death at night.

I take out the tattered, strained map yet again, trying to decode while walking. On the impregnated sheets of paper droplets appear, as if I was walking in the rain, only in this case, not even an umbrella would help. Not like I brought an umbrella either way. My boots thud on the loamy ground, surprisingly solid for now, my sweater is drenched from the humid air. Landscape woods, I notice suddenly, as I arrive at a moderately sized tract of man-planted pine forest. The typical and well-known fungal infection had already begun to make most trees wither away, and the foliage is the very color of rust. The corridors between the evenly planted trees are downright haunting in the mist.

I put the map away. I start walking in between the trees, if everything works out (as it probably won't), I should be able to reach the red-marked trail without any serious issue if I head East. That is, if the way I'm going is even near East, I don't have a compass, and I don't see where the Sun is, either. Between the pines (Austrian pine, I determine by the fir needles on the ground) there are no sounds. I recoil as I notice that the birdsong, which had been quiet to begin with, is now completely gone, and so is the hum of the foresters' machinery, or of the nearby road; in summary, the sounds of general industry in the area have also been shredded into tiny pieces by the Austrian pines' binate swords.

I sit atop a small hump (after confirming that it is not an anthill), and I don't even know why, but I lighten up ever so slightly. I eat my sandwich: white cheddar and Hungarian sausage on rye, cherry tomatoes from a plastic box as sides. The sky is not visible, and neither are any landmarks. I don't see animals at all either, and practically any undergrowth is lacking as well. Only the trees are present beside me. With reinvigorated strength, I begin walking again.

I want to take the map out again, but it isn't there. I can't even begin to comprehend what's happening, but at once, I'm moving by myself, beyond any need for a map or a sandwich, and I wouldn't want to use a compass even if I could. There is one direction here, and that's forward, if I were to turn, I'd expect to face the local alternative for a Minotaur, its head might be a Eurasian boar instead of a bull, just to stay geographically faithful.

My legs are toting me forward, one moment I'm almost flying, while during some steps I feel as if I'm knee-deep in the tallowy podzol. In front of me, I notice a spot of light, just as dim, grey, and moist as the sky.

I'll arrive at my destination soon.

I don't exactly know where that might be, though. It's not about that anymore, I've ceased to be the responsible, well-prepared hiker, I am the Primary Man, who lives in correlation with nature and nobody else. As if I had been the one planting this foothold of a forest decades ago, and as a sign of its gratitude, it's now guiding me out from its Labyrinth. Everything fits perfectly. Or it would.

At the edge of the forest, I regain control of my movements once again, as I get scared and stop in my tracks. A quite steep slope stands in my way, almost like a fracture in the terrain. Down below, however, I finally see something promising: road. Just as unfriendly as the ones before. I want to look at the map to see where I am, but I can remember misplacing it a while ago. Then I notice that I'm still holding it in my left hand. The creased piece of paper stares back at me with hostility.

I put the map away, and take out the binoculars. I look downwards, in the direction of the road, enhancing it just a bit, then I notice the little white-red brush strokes on one of the bare trees. I put the binoculars away, and only now do I look towards the sky.

At the far side of possible perception, the edge of the fog, something looms, in pastel yellow and roseate. Something emanates the strange light, but I'm absolutely sure that the Sun is currently somewhere behind me – that can't be it. Maybe something is burning, but no flames I know would go this high. There are no people in sight. Something is very wrong here, the lights loom over the scenery from what seems to be the stratosphere. I want to take my phone out to take a picture, but then I decide not to. Maybe the magic of it all would disappear completely. I'm fully aware that I'm a part of something abnormal now.

I suddenly notice that the lights are moving, blanketing a little, dark spot, which is probably a village, and I begin to laugh cheerfully. I have no clue for how long I was in the forest, I'm completely unwilling to take my phone out and check, and I've never been a big fan of watches. But here, in the direct neighborhood of something extremely irregular, I, the one who finally knows the direction he's headed in, am the most powerful creature in this world. The light keeps on moving, not necessarily towards me, but indirectly it does get a bit closer to this place as well. I don't worry. Finally, at least for a little while, everything is in order.

I take a deep breath, zip my backpack shut, put it on properly, and look towards the red-marked road. The way down is steep, almost vertical at places, and the only thing to grasp is the loamy wall itself, but I'm not afraid for my hands' cleanliness anymore. Eventually, I'll get down there, one way or another.

Auntie Juci Versus Bentham

Auntie Juci from Tápiószentmárton used to be my grandmother's sister until she passed away from sudden, but not unexpected heart failure about five years ago. Her home was the most disgusting house I have ever had the displeasure of being in: since she was a compulsive chainsmoker, there was a positively constant, visible layer of smoke in every room, and on every surface, a yellowish tint. Her kitchen was constantly covered in grime that smelled as empty energy drink cans on roadsides often do. The garden, however, was huge, with lush greenery; several fruit trees with birds nesting nearby – next to them, forgotten, decades-old rusty gardening tools. Just talking about it, I can almost hear the trashy folk music softly, as if from the background (the kind my older cousins used to put on all the time), and I can feel the inexplicable oil trickling out of the mess of a pizza from the local diner, sticking to the back of my throat.

Auntie Juci was above it all, that's something I had been convinced of quite early in my childhood, at the age of nine. It was one of the rare occasions of just the two of us communicating – she was mostly inside the house, while I spent my time outside, just to avoid having to see, smell or touch the interior.

On the porch – a fair common ground between two worlds – she asked me out of the blue, whether I wanted to see something interesting. Not being wary of her yet, I said yes; she then pulled her translucent plastic pag of self-rolled cigarettes out of her pocket, and without hesitation, grabbed one and ate it whole. After only two chews, she swallowed, while I was just sitting there, speechless, staring at her with surprised disgust. She then looked at me, right in my eyes, and said:

"It's very important for you to know, boy, that no matter what anyone says, in the end, you are right to do whatever you want to."

I have remembered this sentence vividly; and then, I did nothing of the sort. Compared to Auntie Juci, whom I'd seen also eat a lizard about two years later, I was in perpetual stillness throughout the entire rest of my life. Although I wasn't there for any other "miracles" of hers, with the aid of my infantile imagination, I had fully convinced myself that she had killed at least once before: and even later, I could not definitely disprove that to myself.

I actually tried asking about it from my grandma a little while after Auntie's death, but she didn't know what I was talking about. Then, after I had awkwardly elaborated, she only made a face rather unbefitting of her usual direct, affable self, and never talked to me about this again. The only other time I brought it up to her, she pretended she couldn't hear me. I never figured out the reason for her dismissiveness, although thinking back, the fact that I don't remember her ever visiting Auntie Juci speaks volumes.

In high school, I went through a really nasty breakup. That's a complete lie, by the way, it was absolutely proper and almost friendly, a little melancholic at most, but considering the state I was in at the time, it just rubbed me in all the wrong ways. It was, admittedly, a horrible time to begin thinking about the piece of advice she gave me years before; it was also when I realized how much of an effect her way of thinking really had on me.

Afterwards, I had decided for about three hours (which is a horrifyingly long time in retrospect) that I would commit homicide with malice aforethought. I suppose I was incredibly lucky that this period of time fell between 11 PM and 2 AM, depriving me of a chance to really do anything in practice, but I did plan everything, writing it down neatly into a txt file. Then I had a quick panic attack over my own workings, deleted the plan, wiped my Trash folder, cried for two hours with sparse breaks, took a sleeping pill, and then it finally got better. Still, I instinctively knew that Auntie was looking up at me from her afterlife, with visible mockery and distrust.

If nothing else, I did vow to stay mad. Being unable to follow in Auntie's grisly footprints, at least this way, I'd entitled myself to be unreasonable, and that was enough recompense for the time being. Oh, and did I fulfill it. The fumes of my unreciprocated anger stayed thick in every closed space I went in, and whatever I touched, my fingertips miscolored, like a Midas of disgust; and blinded by my belief of being misunderstood, I couldn't see who I was becoming.

In November of the same year, I asked for forgiveness by chance. At a party where we were both present, I just blurted it all out: not the murderous intent and the loathing, but all the evidence proving to myself just how petty I had been for months. I apologized for all of it being awkward, and explained how it was all my fault, then we talked about how it was almost nothing anyway, and how totally over it we both were. A semi-calculated, long-term solution – I definitely wasn't, and in self-defense, I assumed I wasn't the only one lying.

For not sticking with the plan, I began justifying my weakness to myself right after, by claiming how not even Auntie Juci would have killed in that situation, how she would have just let it go... then, for the first time, all at once, I truly saw her for what she had always been. Not the pinnacle of independence, not the inexplicable and unpredictable force of nature I thought of her as. Just an old, wizened incarnation of loathing everything, everyone and especially herself. She was no anti-consequentialist, no free spirit, just a terrifyingly sad old woman driven by a single emotion. Even then, on the porch, she had only wanted to scare me, I think, or enthrall me in her twisted way. Me, the loosely related kid she had nothing to do with.

So at dusk, on the couch of the party's organizer, with the knowledge of what I believed in that moment to be everything, I fell asleep. I was calm and content, having convinced myself that all, including myself, was fine. Then, bafflingly, I even believed it.

Epilogue

I never understood why her flat was divided into rooms clearly discernible by color; whether she liked it that way, or if it was just how the decor happened to be. It could have been accidental. It could also have been Great-grandpa, quite a while ago. The tiny toilet is coral, the dining room predominantly green, the bathroom blue, and the kitchen an old off-white color. The main room (living room and bedroom all at once), is red. The walls have the sort of once-white wallpaper with protruding floral motifs that disappear over time, and so what remains dominant is the color of the carpet, the rosewood bed frame, the fabric of the chair. All red, or almost. The blinds are the only things that don't belong, far too industrial for the style, not fitting in with either the graceful pre-war elegance or the shabby utilitarianism of the 1970s Hungary. The shutters are lowered, and so, the redness cannot escape.

This way, even her almost caricatural paleness disappears in here; her cheeks seem to gather the slightest of flush, her strictly silver-white hair appears darker, the way it might have been about 20 years ago; closer to how it looks like on the only photo there is of her from her youth. She had already had a child when the photo was taken: she was 19. Wild. Even so, nowadays, as she hardly ever leaves the room, even that short-lived liveliness is fading away, fast. Since the last time I met her, about a month ago, everything had somehow managed to get a lot bleaker. It's as if she had merged with her chair, her fragile frame having seemingly fused with the red fabric inside the cocoon of pristinely clean blankets and towels; all sustained by her daughter, my grandmother.

Great-grandma is 88 now. She had aged quite nicely, appearance-wise: despite the trenches of wrinkles, the smile lines around her mouth are still visible. She simply has a kind face. Altogether, she definitely looks good for her age; she also just called me by my uncle's name two times since I have been here. Having only said my own name once, and that having happened right when I arrived, I guess her statistics could be better. Though there are not a lot of common traits between me and him, I do look a lot like he did at my age. But that's not the point: when I'm here, I'm clearly not myself anyway. I act as a full-grown, serious adult, and an uncharacteristically kind fellow simultaneously. Not only because I need the validation (although I do), but because she truly deserves the best, and there is no point in acting flawed. She wouldn't realize it anyway. Being this way relaxes me, and through it, simply my presence should relax her as well. Truly symbiotic.

I glance at the TV as I get back from the kitchen, bringing us a cup of water each. The black box hasn't been turned on in weeks. She still stares at it, either entranced or simply contemplative, exactly like a perplexed songbird. I usually don't like the simile "bird-like, " because it can only remind me of her. She's a lot like a sparrow, both in appearance and manner – small and neutral; aware and silent. Now that the awareness is almost fully gone, she is more like a pet turtle, but that may only cross my mind because of the surreal amount of bed-linen under her, and even more in her lap. They could probably serve as a shell from any looming threats. Maybe they already do.

I put the cup on the coffee table by her side, and sit down on the bed, opposite her. Our conversation so far had mostly been about why people are evil, and how much that sucks for everyone involved. What we haven't done is look for reasons, but she had never been the philosophical type, only someone with firm political beliefs of pacifism and... well, I'm not sure about the rest, and honestly, I probably don't want to figure it out. I know who she voted for. Her views are probably just as outdated. She won't bring them up until I ask, and that, I won't do. I couldn't take the disillusionment. Suddenly, unprompted, she begins talking, as if awoken from a daze (which could very well be the case):

Back when I was a girl... where I went to school, to the next town over, which used to be the same size as our village before they built the railway, and they only connected that one, not ours... they also built a school alongside it. For the families of the railway employees. So, there was this other girl, one who went to the same class... She was really snobbish, you know. Gave herself airs. A really... a pretty Jewish girl, she was. Also very rich. Her father was this medicine manufacturer, or something. You could figure their names out if you asked around there, I think, in the Government Bureau. Just down the ro–"

She hesitates, as if doubting herself. She's right to do so. The village and the town she's talking about are both hundreds of kilometres away. She suddenly slaps her forehead lightly – it seems as though she realises, this time, but she doesn't go on. I cannot be sure.

"I don't think it's th–"

"It's not there, sorry. I know." She gives me an exasperated little smile. The glint in her eyes conveys some pride, but mostly a few seconds of disappointed self-awareness.

"You could still find it, though, probably. But... this... she had a lot of siblings as well. At least three, but more, I think. Of course, that was only outlandish for rich ones like them. The Baron Perényi, who owned the castle and most land around the village only had two, for example. But I was an only child... I had none, somehow. Cousins, many. But maybe... I think it was my father's health. He was a sickly man, bad laborer as well, they said. He used to give me and my friends puppet shows... From behind an old barrel. The same one two kids got sick from playing in, I think. There was insecticide in it for a long time. Just cooking and spewing, out in the sun... But great for shows."

Although she is becoming increasingly incoherent, I feel no need to butt in. She will get back on track, I assume. Most of the time she does, when telling a story. Her gaze darts around, then fixates on me, as I smile reassuringly. For half a second, she looks at me in a way I can't quite place – like paintings do, sometimes. As if she was only a depiction of reality. Then (quite unlike paintings) she opens her mouth, slowly, as the worm of words inches further and further out.

"M-My father loved me more than anything. I had no siblings, so there was only me. The... the girl, though, where was I? What was her name? She had four siblings. And they took them all away. She was a pretty, really... a little snobby, and smug, but with this beautiful black hair... and then she got taken away. Her brothers and sisters too. It was before the Russians... no, yes, the Germans were the ones, they put them in the... they had to board the train and the adults waved them goodbye, and we would never see them again. They were killed. They were all killed and we never saw them, none of us, never."

So far, she was mostly staring into her lap, but now her gaze is piercing. Terrified. Enlightened. She knew all of this once, she had realized it before too, and now here she is, anew facing the thought of the black-haired Jewish girl being gone. Great-grandma had dark hair too, once. I can't help but imagine the girl in the story a little bit like that single old photo of her, from almost seventy years ago. Somehow, there's nothing else I can really, truly understand from what she's saying. I know what she's referring to, and in a different context, I'd be the one lashing out at those who don't feel such events' weight. Yet, there's nothing I can really comprehend now. I take a peek at the photo behind her, feeling like it's staring at me. To my surprise, she, the present her, follows my eyes.

In hers, there is nothing but terror. She does not recognize who it is in the photograph. She mutters something, maybe a prayer, but I can't make anything out. The adrenaline is thumping inside my head and inside my chest, I can feel it in my fingers. Meagerly, she lifts her right arm up halfway, as if to point somewhere, then decides not to, after all. Then, she lowers her face again, and stops talking entirely. In the complete silence only broken up by the unoiled ticking of the fancy bird-motif clock, I quickly text my grandma to come over, since I feel far from equipped to handle the situation.

When I hear the doorbell ring and get up to open the door, her head perches up, and she says, in an unfittingly coarse voice, "In the end, it will go the same way, right? For me. I'm... how old I am doesn't matter all that much, if we're honest. I just noticed, barely." She lets out a little, cheerful chuckle, and somehow, well before opening the door for my grandma, I know that this would be her last sentence to me.

It was, and then I never met her again. I kept the photo, though.

Approved by the Environmental Protection Agency

In a depressing line, like the starting boxes on a greyhound racetrack, decay the tumbling garages addressed to the once-privileged, erstwhile assigned to those who used to hold whatever miniscule positions of power had been available within housing estates from the Eastern Bloc. Now, their descendants do not park cars inside. The new kinds of machines probably wouldn't fit anyway; but disregarding the size, the main reason for its abandonment is still the heavily present issue of asbestos, elegantly transfused into the thin tin of the roof. Apart from rusting Wartburgs, not much is stored inside any of them anymore; ironically, what they're actually commonly used for is hoarding the unwanted, ever-so-slightly sentimental objects of dead grandparents or other relatives; objects which do not hold such value to anyone living, but rather become sentimental in their own right through years of use and conjoinment. Great-grandma's tattered, proudly ugly but highly functional "antique" tablecloth; Grandpa's lamp which the whole family knows could have exploded at any moment.

The garages are, altogether, an eyesore, they are only still standing here because looking at the corroding, neglected railways is even worse. Still, if someone lives anywhere higher than the second floor, they can still clearly see it from their back windows, indirectly making their lingering a dubious privilege to the few people spread across a few flats. The straight-line they form does not break – the grey ceilings form a continuous, sidewalk-like platform. It remains seemingly infinite, with the flyover to the north just barely visible. I climb atop a garage, nevermind the asbestos shards now comfortably sitting in my palm, just barely piercing the skin. A true supervillain origin story: I am poisoned; I will become venomous.

Maybe even this wasteland would be better, I think, looking over to the overgrown greenery on the other side of the rails – not a train in sight. That first remark is not true, by the way, the hairs suddenly stand up on my back, just imagining getting stuck in the impenetrable bushland, with the thorns and heroin needles piercing my skin more than the microscopic, poisonous shards ever would (I actually have no clue about whether people even use heroin in there, but I'm currently not feeling like not making assumptions, and if I was a heroin user, I sure as hell would do it inside some bushes). It's cold and now my palms hurt. The repetitive howling is nearly unbearable. It's not like a dog, necessarily, more like a machine consciously created to sound similar to one. I don't know where it's coming from, the sound is delocalized and distant, creating overall dizziness. That might actually be due to the cold, now that I think about it. I forgot to bring a hat.

The day is dark, the sky is grey, and I keep on forgetting where and when I had come from. The wind is blowing past my ears. Of course, I was the one who chose to climb on top of an old garage. Leaving this place is probably the only reasonable choice if nobody is around. The people have disappeared, sublimated while out of focus, rapidly photoshopped from the picture taken with my perception's lens, like unnecessary background characters. At the edge of my vision, though, the buildings still stare, their whole existence slightly grotesque without anyone to populate their surroundings. There is presumably nobody inside, either: I've tried ringing a few doorbells.

To begin my preparation before the inevitable descent, I turn around with haste, spinning on my heel; the roof picks this exact moment to finally give up, crumbling beneath my left foot, the plastic walls caving in on the mass amassed within, which now includes me despite my heavy opposition to this fact (looks like the only quality components in this structure were the screws holding the roof to the walls all along, still holding out, making the whole situation all the more dangerous via their functionality). Inside is a gob of matter: people-matter, which I am currently in the center of. Its parts look content enough, obliviously remaining real despite the absurd situation. I try to pull my leg out of several things at once, from the oozing blob and the roof alike; the latter of which I now feel an inexplicable urge to lick. I finally manage to stumble out, scraping and splitting my trousers open on the road, as the garage suddenly realizes the basic rules of physics regarding an abundance of nondescript material in a place it shouldn't rationally fit into, but, instead of expectedly exploding, promptly disappears.

I walk over to the playground with a dinosaur-shaped jungle gym, and sit down on a bench, disoriented. I think of picking up a considerably large rock and breaking one of the glass doors leading into any of the buildings, just to escape the cold, but the urge to do nothing easily crushes the yearning for taking action, so I just keep on sitting. I don't know how and when my face gets buried in my palms, but here we go, I guess. I'm shivering already. Somehow, I know it will freeze tonight, maybe the temperature already is below zero. I decide to lie down on the bench. The wood comforts me as I close my eyes trying to ignore the futility of any possible action. The howling is back: it's not at all louder, but I instinctively know that it's coming from directly next to my ears now, and I have not been more sure about anything before, than what I suddenly grasp, reluctantly stubborn: that I won't open my eyes, no matter what or why.

Indoors Balcony

On the balcony; if it can even be considered that. A gallery with a low handrail – the kitchen directly underneath. Below: glimmering. Dark blue and magenta lines of colour and light, entangling the table and the kitchen in a particular way, brightening the bags of chips and the empty bottles. From where we are, the light's source is not visible, giving it all a sort of synthwave-otherworldly aesthetic.

It's half past three AM. Many are sleeping, the others have scattered into groups of two and three. Someone is inside the upper floor bathroom.

In Tódor Valla's hand there is a glass, quarter full of some beverage, nearly empty for almost an hour now. Radószky's crossed arms, in the shape of an "X," an unmistakably negative answer, end in empty hands.

"All I'm saying is," Valla says, "that if I were to climb down there, or so help me God, jump, the chance of me getting hurt is really close to zero."

"There are glass bottles down there, Tódor, for fuck's sake. If you were to jump on about eight empty bottles that are standing on an unstable wooden table, you think you'd just get up, unscathed? Come on."

"We are not that high up. We aren't high up at all. We are not even a little high up. Look," Valla says, putting his glass down onto the handrail's flat, top part: the handrail that would probably bring comfort to most people, but there isn't much in Radószky's mind right now except for the lack of that feeling, a sense of security (not her own, to be fair), as she steps closer to Valla. He, as if he hadn't even noticed her at all, is wondering about the simplest way to climb atop a relatively tall barrier, which, perhaps, wasn't only made with a decorative intent (the probable intended secondary function could have been preventing drunk youngsters from falling to their doom). All that with a wobbly head and legs that don't provide full stability. Or vice versa.

"Tódor. Don't even think about climbing up there, alright? I believe you, okay? I believe you. I believe that you could easily fall head-first onto that table, and you know what, I believe that you would even fucking dare to do it. But please, don't climb. Because I'm the only one here. And you know I've never been the best at stopping people from... doing stuff."

Valla sits down. His glass is left on the handrail – nobody had noticed yet (except for the house's only, currently sleeping, present resident) that because of the architects' whims there is underfloor heating even on top of the barrier. Therefore, Valla's drink will likely soon be boiled, seethed and mulled to the point of being undrinkable (not that the heating is that strong, but it surely won't be part of the gladly consumable category).

"Do you actually think this is about whether I'm brave enough?"

Radószky had always been considered "pretty good with people," which basically meant that she could read obvious signs quite fast and with ample self-confidence. This was, for instance, a direct cause for a worried look and to instantly sit in front of Valla, cross-legged, seemingly relaxed, but ready to dart ahead, if necessary. She observes the silence. After a while, Valla continues.

"It's not like I actually want to jump down, though. Intrusive thoughts, you know them, those happen to anyone. I don't have anything apart from that going on. But... what effect do you think it'd have on the world? Would it really have any at all? What would happen if I were to survive, and what if I died, just like you said?"

"Both would suck."

"Yeah, fair. If I were to survive, do you think they'd blame you?"

"Well, should that be the case, I hope you wouldn't say that it was me who pushed you."

"But if I died, then for sure. You would be, like, the prime, number one suspect."

"Do you think they would believe that a girl who's forty-five kilograms with the scale included could push you over an eighty centimetres tall, thick barrier?"

"I dunno. People are dumb."

Silence. Neither is looking at the other. Meanwhile, somewhere else, two other people have gone to sleep, but these and those two don't notice each other in any way.

"The saddest part is that I don't care."

Radószky's head perks up. Uh-oh. Bad train of thought.

"I mean, I'm sorry, but if I died, I wouldn't really care, I think. But I'll say it again if you want me to, I don't want that to happen. Actually, I don't even feel like not wanting to live. I sort of enjoy life nowadays. But, really, I wouldn't mind kicking the bucket. Even though I feel good. I don't hate myself. I don't hate anyone. But I still can't bring myself to care. You know why?"

Radószky inches closer. Valla notices, but doesn't say anything, and Radószky knows that.

"Because in the grand scheme of things, it wouldn't matter a lot. It wouldn't carry that great of a weight. Think about it, if I died, like this, suffering among shards of glass, and what's more, a friend of mine would be suspected of murder because of me, who would that matter to? You, and other friends, and my parents. But just how many people are these, and how long would it take until I were completely forgotten?"

"Okay, Tódor, you're not only drunk, but clichéd as well. I don't mind your monologuing, but... at least do it in a way that makes sense."

Valla suddenly stands up, but doesn't move from where he'd been sitting. Despite the overbearing amount of adrenaline released into her system, Radószky, slowly and frigidly, stands up as well. Valla waits until she's on her feet, then looks into her eyes, and with an unsure, yet somewhat robotic motion of his arm, pushes the glass onto the table down below. Clattering: that's what one would expect, but the only audible sound is a single, strong and sudden one, like splashing water and the crash of two porcelain matchboxes at the same time. Glass eggs on the side of the bowl.

"Jesus. What the hell? You'll clean that up, right?"

"Of course, sure. I was just testing something."

Someone turns in their sleep in the living room. A girl leaves the bathroom, but doesn't look in their direction. The suspenseful silence ends simultaneously with the toilet's automatic exhaust fan, as Valla speaks up:

"If they couldn't hear this at all, would they hear me landing, like, immediately?" seeing Radószky's increasingly frightened expression, he adds "As I've said, this is all hypothetical. I really am alright, except for the daybreak drunkenness and the existential crisis."

"If this is all hypothetical, then I'd be glad if we, say, hypothetically went downstairs, or hypothetically away from this barrier, or if you would hypothetically stop talking about plummeting head-first into a table."

"The funny part is that I still think I'd probably be alright."

"Nothing's funny about that. Let's go downstairs. I don't like this, and I genuinely don't know why you're taking your issues out on me."

"Just a second, I'm gonna get to the point I wanted to arrive at. Please, tell me, if I were to jump from here and survive, but suffer some serious injuries, how much would you hate me then? Let's say I became mute, or got paralyzed completely, or went braindead or into a coma, and I couldn't prove your innocence, and neither could you, not completely, at least... Obviously, everyone would both think and say 'surely not,' but nobody'd be absolutely certain. And I'd just lie there, hooked up to all sorts of machines, having crippled not only myself, but maybe your future too. How much would you despise me? Would you come visit? Me, the one who had maimed two people because of a momentary idiotic burst of apathy-filled brooding? And if you did, how often would you think about turning the machines off, as to finish what I had begun doing to myself?"

Radószky doesn't answer.

Someone has switched off the blue-magenta lights downstairs, and the lower floor's now cloaked itself in an insinuating semidarkness, which, due to a complete lack of inside lighting, can only be attributed to the neighbor's porch lamp and the buzzing street LED-s.

Triumph

The small kitchen windows of hundreds of flats on the opposite side of the circular gallery blink as a pulse, whenever one turns dark, another seems to light up in an instant, then all over again somewhere else. The quadrangle separating me from that side is not wide enough for the plants in the middle to receive enough light. In twenty-one hours of an average spring day, they're completely blocked from sunlight by the six-story, rectangular buildings. I'm up top, floor six; some incredible comedic clairvoyant had crudely carved a blocky nine after the number six inside the elevator. Half of the flats up here don't even get the amenity of a balcony. I know for a fact that the one I'm trying to enter, my reluctance increasing by the minute, does not. So I keep staring at the feeble bushes and the mushy, green weeds in place of what may once have been grass, when I hear the door behind me unlock. I've just been starting to wonder whether I should ring the doorbell again. It isn't broken, I could clearly hear the shrill noise from right above the door's inside half, but whoever was home had so far shown the same reluctance to let me in as I had to even come here.

She only opens the thin plastic door to an angle of about thirty degrees. It's Anna. If it came down to my fight or flight response, I would never have survived in the wilderness. So all I do is stand there as all my muscles tense up at the same time, though not tight enough for it to be visible, I think. She's in "home clothes," slippers and sweatpants and a worn-out T-shirt. I can't quite interpret the look in her eyes, and I silently continue to decipher, until she speaks.

"Well?"

"Uh." I half-succeed to gather myself. "Hi, hello. Are your parents..."

I pause at the end. I hope she'll get what I mean; I hope it's what I mean that she'll think she gets.

"Mom's at the hospital, filling some stuff out. Dad's at Aron's place, moving things back and forth and whatnot. So I'm the one bearing the burden of responsibility right now. Homeowner and security."

She leans against the doorframe, her arms loosely crossed, one of the slippers moving rhythmically back and forth through the air. An adult, I realize again. More than me, at least. Her stance is clearly guarded, yet confident, or she may be communicating this deliberately. I still can't find my way around the conversation, and her aim seems to be to maintain this status quo.

"Well, I just wanted to make sure they know that I'm ready to share anything if they ask me to."

"Oh, yeah?" For a second, her vigilant glare gives way to something else. Then again, I may be projecting.

"Yeah. Alex's things. He had a lot, you know that. I mean, like, within him. You know."

***

Alex was seventeen when they admitted him. The same goes for today, as far as I know – it has only been around two weeks. He gave a huge part of his belongings away, he does not have a lot of things in a physical sense, only a lot of them going on. It was only a few days before he left that I had been in his room. Its dark blue walls made the interior seem smaller than it already was; the space left by Aron's (why their parents gave them all names beginning with "A" still manages to confuse me) bed and furniture emptier than ever, Alex's once crammed overhead bookshelf now gap-toothed; his wardrobe standing like an ancient monument on the long stretch of wall opposite the door. I remember the soft afternoon light dispersed by my half-liter green bottle of a sugar-free soft drink, coating the room. The two of us, quietly concentrating, were playing some bootleg nineties racing game on his SNES that he got for his birthday in January, from me. He beat me every single time. It was the only two-player game that he had.

That was a Saturday. Next Tuesday, he didn't come to school. Then they took him to the local children's hospital – at 17, it was still not the adults' psych ward where they locked him up.

His dad told me that Alex hadn't even tried anything, that he, without a word, had hopped on a bus and gone to a nearby quarry, that he had purchased a gun from somewhere but hadn't fired it once. In the old man's words, "he gave it to me on his own. The police are gonna know a lot better what to do with that." Incidentally, Alex had never liked cops all that much.

***

"I brought back the books that he gave me." I say. "He'd probably want them back, now that it's all turned out like this."

She is staring a hole into where my eyes are supposed to be, waiting. She is uncaring and unmoved by my own troubles. She is positioned above all, a different person entirely from who she used to be just a little while ago. She is shivering slightly – by now, the sun has gone down completely, and unlike me, she has no coat on, nor a knapsack full of books to warm her backside.

"I just wanna... Put them on his shelves. Or his uh, desk. Maybe organize it a bit, while I'm at it... Could you let me in, for just a few minutes?"

"No, actually, I could not."

"Yeah. Okay." I briefly pause here, just now processing the information. "Why, exactly?"

She raises her eyebrows, more troubled than amused: in genuine disbelief. A black puddle starts to form somewhere deep inside me, as I realize with dread that it is her answer that I'm dreading in the first place.

"That's not a real question, right? I mean, is it? I'm actually curious now." She shivers again, her face contorted into a forced grin, and now the initial self-confidence shows itself to be a clear fabrication. For a short second, I've managed to look behind the veil of her persona, but it's too late now. The dark muck is clouding my perception, her words dimmed by the viscous partition it produces to ensure my safety. She's extremely high-strung; I am downright terrified. Scared stiff by the chance of having to face the consequences of my actions.

"Haven't I apologized? I have, haven't I?" My voice could be coming from the bottom of a lake, and it wouldn't make that big of a difference. The cold sensation in the back of my neck does not cease; the malicious feelings are coming alive inside the pit in my stomach.

"Yes, you have. That was nice of you. I mean that. But you can't just–"

Even in this situation, she is incredibly attractive. I hate this. If not for that, I would have left already, and I'm disgusted with myself. Her entire demeanor is a shifting mess of confusion and anger and incredible composure, but she is still here. Time to ruin it all. But maybe, even this is a way of weaseling myself out of this situation – pretending not to be in control. Wait...

"Look, I want nothing to do with you. That's it, man. I don't care for you, alright? I'm not mad, but I don't have the slightest inclination to associate with you." No way to stop the surge of memories now, I guess. Her voice shakes slightly, but I can't hear the rest either way.

***

The same Sunday, in the same room, the same place where I had spent the majority of my afternoon, I kiss her. There is not enough light to create the sort of show, as with the soda bottle earlier. Four wine flasks are laying around, all empty, but they are too polished to do anything of the sort. A glass has been knocked over, sour aroma rises from the carpet. The music's ended, Alex is probably smoking outside with some of our mutual friends who still haven't gone home... That all goes through my head for the few seconds it lasts, and then suddenly it doesn't anymore.

"I... That was cool." I chuckle, as her head tilts back slightly.

"Yeah..." she goes deep into thought. "I just don't give a shit anymore, man. Alright, it was uh. Alright."

I know of nothing but life at that moment. It has been a while since I've felt this happy, and the alcohol and the arousal and her body's warmth mix and mash inside my heart and lungs, condensed into pure vitality. I breathe in, deep,

44

my soul cleaner than it had been for such a long time it seems surreal.

"No more wine, huh."

"Probably no need form... For more. I think we shu-should go the, just go back to the people and uh..." she slurs, and pauses. I wait patiently, still grinning in bliss and the full awareness of eventual oblivion. Then, as she looks into my eyes with urgency, I quickly support her to the toilet and let her friend, the one who has the dubious title of "our very own teetotaler," help her out with puking. For a minute, I remain close by, then as I hear her still vomit, I put on my coat and slip away without a single word.

***

"Look, I just wanna organize his things and–"

"Literally, fuck off. Please! I don't wanna be like this with you right now, but you have to understand. Leave."

"I can prove that it's not about you. You can be outside or whatever."

She laughs, the noise sharp and sudden enough to pierce through my defenses. This single moment of self-awareness stops my brain in its tracks completely.

"Do you hear yourself?" I know I do not. "That's crazy, those are the words of a goddamn lunatic. Listen to me! Listen to yourself!"

"I apologized. I have." I stumble over my words, my ears ringing. "And, like, you know, that's... I know I was an asshole, and I'm sorry. I shouldn't have left, and I shouldn't have gotten... It shouldn't have gotten to that point. But the fact is that nothing really happened, you know."

"I mean, that depends on what you define as nothing, I guess. You didn't rape me, that's really fucking great, y'know, you really did a nice job there... And I guess you didn't even touch me anywhere inappropriate, also wonderful to know, though to be fair, we both know that we don't know for sure," I want to interlude with the idea that I would have probably remembered that happening, but even in the state I'm in, I instinctively realize that to shut up is the best course of action here, "but here's the thing: I don't remember anything, at all. You got me... Or at least, before you start the word-splitting game, we got me blackout drunk, and you took advantage of that. That's the bottom line, man. It could have been worse, but that doesn't change the fact that you suck. I've already told you I don't care anymore, but you also can't just pretend that everything is like it once was. Go away."

I'm unsure what she thinks is going on inside my head – that I don't know that? I'm aware, now more than ever before, and it's suffocating. And I know I can't just keep denying everything, but I also can't get over the impossibility of making it right instantly. I can't just leave. That would spell defeat, something I couldn't take right now. And, even so, haven't I repented enough? I felt like shit for so long. I still do. What more does she expect? I can headbutt the metal windowsill, or all of them if that's how I make things go back to neutral. I could throw the books down all six stories.

Better yet, I could just mess everything up. I could end this conversation once and for all. At the moment, it still seems better than admitting the fact that I've lost; despite the rational parts of my mind screaming against it in unison, their cries are drowned out by the seas and sinkholes of the black substance of unjustified frustration that finally manages to topple my brain.

"You know..." I begin with a sense of suspect resignation, my words tangled, "I heard that you and Aron are organizing something again, right here. So, for that, I mean, you don't have to let me inside now, but then could you invite me for that, maybe, when it comes?"

In an instant, things shift. She is not shocked, but suddenly looks simply so very tired. She says nothing and does not move inside the slightest, just gazes at me with her dazzling, exhausted eyes. I leave silently, and hurry down the stairs without any sensation, or emotion. Only when looking back at the front view of the house, do I feel something flicker within me, as I notice the lack of balconies on the sixth floor, and remember how I promised the others that I would bring Alex's weed that he keeps in his desk drawer. It seems so distant from real life, yet even so, I suddenly get an inkling of understanding as to why he had left. Still, I know nothing and understand nothing. All that remains is the recognition of the fact that I'm never coming back.

A huge additional thank you to Dalma Szentpály, an incredible mentor and much-needed editor-in-chief, to Tündi Antalik for the continued support and the cover art, to Miki Góczán for doing actual graphic design in my stead, to Andris Csontos and Beni Hajdu for their regular quality-checks, and (naturally) to my family for all the incredible support.

Additional editing by Dalma Szentpály

Cover art by Tünde Antalik

Cover design by Miklós Góczán